FROM BEYOND

THE BEYOND

BOOK ONE

ANDREW DAVIE

Dedicated to

*The Three Horsemen of Hong Kong, Mojo, Yumi, O'Brien, Mr. Sandwich,
The Golden Girl, and The Next Generation of Davie Bros.*

SOUTH CHINA SEA, 1875, AFTERMATH OF THE SECOND OPIUM OR ARROW WAR

"SWITCH TO CHAIN SHOT!"

The command had cut through the smoke and could be heard above the wails. The sound of clanking metal then completely replaced voices as the ever-loyal crew shoved the iron orbs into the breeches and lit the cannon's fuses. There was a brief moment of quiet, which was followed by concussive bursts that shattered the silence. They echoed from underneath the deck and lurched the boat toward the port side. The men braced themselves for the wrath of inertia. The ship, a rugged looking merchantman named *"The Ajax"*, which had seen better days, buckled but maintained her composure.

Declan Malcolm watched the payload arc across the sky, followed by the faint glow of phosphorous residue, and tear into the foresail of the enemy ship. Malcolm was as thin as a reed, but his muscles were defined. He turned the wheel and felt the boat cut through the water; the veins on his arms practically burst through his skin. It took almost all of this effort to fight against the water's current, but he was successful.

He smelled the sulfur from the cannons and barked out orders for the men to get ready to board the enemy ship once

1

they had made contact. Saltwater sprayed his face and stung his cuts which never seemed to heal. Beneath him, the crew continued to feed the cannons for their assault. The men would have followed Malcolm into the depths of Hades. As he thought of the fires of Hell, Malcolm reflected on the chain of events that led him here.

A famine had forced an exodus from their home in the countryside, and Malcolm's young bride had grown deathly ill during the journey. They had weathered the epidemic for as long as it was possible and had subsisted on virtually nothing until they sought salvation elsewhere.

He and his wife boarded a train and went to London. Though they had no connections, they finally found refuge, living in squalor amongst a collection of three other families. Each night Malcolm would hold his wife close to him, drag a washcloth over her forehead, and soothe her fever. It eventually got to the point where he could feel her bones protrude through her skin. She could barely speak; words would drip from her mouth in hushed tones. She was discolored, pale, and sapped of all strength. The priest had offered absolution for her, but Malcolm's wife continued to live.

Malcolm worked nearly twenty hours a day in the slaughterhouse, collapsing the skulls of cloven-hoofed animals. He spent his time praying to a God he had trouble believing in anymore. The repetition without reprieve eventually eroded Malcolm's will. Rampant disease among the cattle brought the factory to a standstill. Unable to provide for his family without a job, he soon took loans which compounded in a short duration. One night, long after the moon had risen, he was visited by the associates of his usurer.

Expertly, they worked him over and enrolled him into debtor's prison. For six long months, he festered inside. He was able to fend off insanity along with most of the predatory advances of other inmates. Malcolm learned of his wife's removal from their home, and her placement in a sanitarium. She still clung to life and would repeat Malcolm's name over again while under the effects of her malaise. The priest gave Malcolm her most treasured belongings, including her locket, with the thought that they would bring Malcolm peace or at least revitalize his endurance. Bordering on the brink and ready to jump willingly into the abyss, ultimately, Malcolm had been rescued by a half Russian expatriate.

The gruff philosopher, Tretiak, taught Malcolm how to handle himself when words alone could no longer work. Tretiak filled Malcolm's mind with abstract philosophies and history. More importantly, he gave Malcolm focus and reminded him of his reasons to leave debtor's prison. Malcolm's release came in the form of the Jameson & Brixton company who, looking for cheap labor, bought his debt. The morning after he was released, he found himself aboard *The Emerald* as an indentured servant. They were going to head for the Orient in hopes of bringing glory to the company in the form of silks and spices.

Malcolm's wife's fate remained unknown to him.

THE RAILWAY STRIKE OF 1877,
PITTSBURGH, PA

RAY RIDLEY MADE HIS WAY TOWARD THE SALOON. Even though it was late in the evening, the sun hadn't fully set since it was July. As he navigated through the throng of people on the sidewalk, he passed by a group of railway workers who had surrounded a brakeman who'd mentioned their wages were going to be cut yet again. Next to the brakeman was a thin fellow in spectacles who was quite the orator. The bespectacled speaker was standing on an apple box which had made him at least a foot taller than the next tallest person in the crowd.

The man talked about class disparity, specifically, the imbalance between them. He clearly had their attention, but he'd obviously studied rhetoric and knew when to lean into a long pause or slam his fist into his hand to make a point. Labor disputes were nothing new, but it seemed like strikes were now distinct possibilities as opposed to idle threats. The financial panic of '73 had triggered "The Long Depression," which had wreaked havoc across the country.

Ridley ducked inside the saloon just as the man had finished making a point that drew applause from the crowd. Ridley could tell the orator was just getting started. While Ridley had never heard this particular speech before, he was familiar with the cadence the man had used. The man had possibly been a fire and brimstone preacher or part of a congregation before he'd gotten involved with the workers.

It was only a matter of time before the workers struck in Pittsburgh. A few weeks previously, workers for the B&O had gone on strike in West Virginia; it was still happening, and there were rumors and talk of strikes happening in New York and Baltimore. While some of these strikes would be peaceful demonstrations, many would not.

THE EMERALD'S CAPTAIN, CHARLES FITZGIBBONS, WAS A runt of a man who'd earned his commission through a family connection. He was incompetent in his position of authority and made mistakes at almost every turn. Collectively, the men loathed him. Months into their voyage, Fitzgibbons developed a case of cabin fever. Somewhere around Cape Horn, he emerged from his quarters, still in his nightgown, and in his delirium shot two of the crew. Fitzgibbons claimed they were minions of Lucifer before he was subdued. The men, already weary from the journey, and suffering painful cramping from various vitamin deficiencies, decided to send Fitzgibbons to Davy Jones Locker. They received temporary relief in the form of retribution when his manacled body broke the water's plane.

Afterward, a maelstrom erupted aboard the ship over the balance of power. Cutlasses were drawn and factions were nominated. The crew, now at the breaking point, were on the verge of complete chaos. Malcolm soon cooled them of their rage, and due to his prowess and proven capabilities in almost every regard, he was nominated for the position of the new captain, much to the chagrin of the first mate. Nearly twice in height and width as Malcolm, the first mate, a hard man named O'Hanlon, challenged Malcolm to a bare-knuckle match for the captaincy and the right to the ship. O'Hanlon's hair was dark red, the color of cinnamon, and he had a braided beard. He took his shirt off and revealed a physique that looked like Raphael or Donatello might have carved it. He was a sight to behold.

"He might be quick with the words, but let's see how quick he is with these," O'Hanlon had said.

With that, he lifted his hands: misshapen and the size of Christmas hams.

"We're out of harm's way. No need to stir up trouble," Malcolm said as he slowly backed from the giant.

"Let's go," O'Hanlon said and put his hands up in the traditional Marquis-of-Queensbury style.

Malcolm attempted to further reason with this behemoth, but to no avail. O'Hanlon had helped himself to a few servings of grog during the brief reign of chaos after the crew had dealt with Fitzgibbons, and this juggernaut would be soothed by no words. The first punch was telegraphed, and Malcolm avoided it, but even in his sorry state O'Hanlon possessed the skills of an excellent pugilist.

It had been rumored O'Hanlon had gone sixty-five rounds with Jem Mace. Of course, there were also rumors he had been the scion of a cattle baron back in the Americas, and that he had previously been a Merchant Marine during the American Civil War. Regardless, Malcolm had misjudged O'Hanlon's ability, and the second punch caught him on the shoulder. Malcolm was knocked to the ground from sheer force.

"Where you going?" O'Hanlon said as Malcolm crab-walked away. "We're only just getting started," O'Hanlon added.

O'Hanlon plodded forth and made a come-hither motion with his fists. Malcolm rose to his feet. He was numb from the blow. However, Malcolm was still agile and nimble. He ducked around the mast and kept enough space between himself and O'Hanlon.

"Quit yer stalling and come take your medicine. This is a stand-down, not some square dance," O'Hanlon said.

The boat had tacked at that moment, and the mast swung directly toward Malcolm who rolled over the top of it and landed on his feet. The move surprised the crew, most of all O'Hanlon, who had let his guard down for a split second. The crew watched aghast as Malcolm cleared the distance between him and O'Hanlon. While Malcolm was undoubtedly a man of honor, this was not a proper match. There was no referee, no judges, and the winner would not get his hand raised at the end. Malcolm spotted a rawhide mallet lying on the deck from when the crew had needed to tend to some carpentry.

Malcolm picked it up and landed a solid shot to O'Hanlon's sternum. The sound resonated throughout the ship like a coconut being split open. O'Hanlon didn't even have time to let out an exclamation. He was unconscious before he hit the ground. His body crumpled, and when he awoke, he would have quite the bruise. A cheer erupted from the crew who, like in the Arthurian legend, had just witnessed their king draw the sword from the stone. A minute or so later, Malcolm helped O'Hanlon onto his feet.

"I'll swear my allegiance to you," O'Hanlon finally managed as the rest of the crew dispersed back to their stations. He repeatedly touched his chest where a knot was beginning to emerge.

"But one day, I'm going to want my rematch."

THE RAILWAY STRIKE OF 1877, PITTSBURGH, PA

RIDLEY WALKED UP TO THE BAR AND ORDERED A whiskey. He drank it quickly and ordered a beer. This one he would drink slowly. As the bartender placed the drink in front of him, Antony Dranoff strode into the saloon.

Even though Dranoff was a few years past his prime, he still carried himself with the air of someone it would be best to avoid in a fight. Dranoff ordered a beer and sat down next to Ridley. While the temperance movement had been gaining traction throughout the country, it had not taken hold in Pittsburgh, and the saloon remained pretty crowded.

"This Thursday, at the end of the workday."

Ridley nodded and sipped his beer. So, Pittsburgh would join in and strike.

"They're bringing in the National Guard," Dranoff added and looked around the bar. He tried to make eye contact with someone. Each time he and Ridley went to a saloon, Dranoff would gauge the room and attempt to get into a skirmish with someone. Of course, Dranoff would have to vet them first. Sometimes, if it was lacking, Dranoff would settle. If it had been up to him, Dranoff would prefer for his opponent to be taller and heavier. It would be the only way to make it fair.

Dranoff had commanded a partisan group for The North during the war which did it all: irregular warfare, reconnaissance, and protection. Their record was impressive, and Dranoff kept a walking stick which he notched to keep track of the lives he'd taken. When Ridley had asked about the number, Dranoff said he'd lost count. Truthfully, Dranoff didn't know what the number had been, but it served as good psychological warfare since the walking stick and notches had become a rumor which festered among Dranoff's enemies. Rather than think about tactics, they were more concerned with avoiding becoming another groove on the handle.

Since Ridley had joined the company, he'd heard a new rumor about Dranoff almost every day. For example, the weapons the man favored. The most recent was he'd taken a rifle that had been blessed by a medicine man during the Apache Wars. The rumor went around the rifle would give Dranoff perfect aim. Ridley would always laugh when he thought of that one since Dranoff's aim was terrible. However, Dranoff was one of the most effective close combat fighters Ridley had ever seen. The man favored a Krag Bowie Bayonet that he kept in his boot. He was lethal with the weapon.

Dranoff was also equally good with his fists. Another rumor circulated he had taken on an entire regiment one at a time. Ridley wouldn't be able to dispute this last one, as it had happened before Ridley had joined. At this point, though, Ridley wouldn't have had trouble believing it after all of the feats he'd seen Dranoff perform.

The last one, probably Ridley's favorite, was Dranoff waged personal war with the Apaches and spent time living like a mountain man. Dranoff would consume the livers of his dead enemies. Of course, in this particular rumor, Dranoff had been confused for Liver-eating Johnson.

THE ENEMY VESSEL HAD MOVED WITH THE OCEAN current but hadn't been able to go very far. Its sails were tattered and beyond any use. It wouldn't be long before Malcolm's crew would be able to board them. The enemy vessel was close enough that Malcolm could hear the cries of the wounded. He attached his fighting iron. Below him, his crew was going through pre-battle rituals: asking for a Deity's blessing, fulfilling a promise to deliver heathens to salvation, and more.

O'Hanlon repeatedly swung his massive shillelagh which was capable of crushing bone. Grid remained stiff, and his mask prevented him from ever having to reveal genuine emotion. One of his leathery hands clutched a tomahawk and the other a serrated knife. Malcolm gave the command to ram the boat, and the crew erupted into a frenzy. The boats collided. Wood splintered, and the sound cracked like lightning. Grappling hooks were cast out like a spider designing a web, and once they had been secured on the edge of the enemy ship, Malcolm's crew inched across. They bore their weapons in their teeth. They were missionaries of doom.

The melee sprang out of the confusion. The men on both sides choked on thick smoke. Both crews intertwined with each other. Malcolm surveyed the commotion from the edge of *The Ajax*. O'Hanlon had been consumed in a blinding rage and bowled over six men. He struck blows with his shillelagh and resembled a golem from ancient lore — a mythical beast who had been conjured and unleashed on the unsuspecting enemy crew. Grid moved like undulating liquid. His hatchet and knife strikes were sometimes too quick for the human mind to process. Often, his opponents would continue to fight even after they had technically been killed. Strange looks appeared on their faces, as to why their bodies had not obeyed commands from their brains; slowly, recognition would replace ignorance as life would leave them.

The tide of the battle turned quickly, and fear spread like a plague. Some took their chances in the water. Other men lost control of themselves. They spoke in tongues and wandered in search of possible sanctuary. When he sensed the enemy's will had been broken, Malcolm called off the dogs. Collectively both crews heaved the bodies of the dead overboard. After he had descended onto the ship, Malcolm made his way toward the captain's quarters. When he was about to turn the handle, the cabin's door opened. From inside the darkness of the captain's quarters, she walked out into the light.

THE RAILWAY STRIKE OF 1877, PITTSBURGH, PA

RIDLEY HAD BEEN A SHARPSHOOTER WHO'D JOINED Dranoff's partisan group, and Ridley's reputation circulated among his enemies as well. Over time, Ridley learned never to debunk any of the rumors which circulated about either him or Dranoff. In fact, he would encourage them whenever he could. It had been rumored he'd once shot a man from one thousand yards with his Whitworth .451.

It had been a shorter distance.

Ridley finished his beer and debated ordering another one. The soldier was probably closer to eight hundred yards away, but Ridley never tried to correct it. Over time, the length continued to grow until it was over a thousand yards. Soon it would be fifteen hundred.

After the war ended, Ridley tried to settle down and make an attempt at farming, but there had been an urge which could only be satiated one way. He knew Dranoff felt similarly, so Ridley sought Dranoff out. The man hadn't been difficult to find. Ridley found him in jail awaiting trial. One of the people at the bar who'd been on the receiving end of one of Dranoff's brawls had been the nephew of a state senator. They were going to make an example out of Dranoff.

SOUTH CHINA SEA, 1875,
AFTERMATH OF THE SECOND
OPIUM OR ARROW WAR

"Three Finger" Tang was a wiry man, almost all sinew, with gray hair, broken teeth, and a left eyelid that drooped. A carved meerschaum dangled from his lips. The smoke from his pipe lingered around the crown of his head like a halo. Tang lived on a collection of sampan boats buried within the Hong Kong harbor along with a multitude of wives and children. He never left his makeshift island. Instead, he would send one of his brood as an emissary to negotiate dealings on his behalf. Though the port was under the protection of Her Majesty's crown, it was Tang who truly controlled everything which entered or exited Hong Kong's harbor.

When *The Emerald* finally arrived in Hong Kong, the men descended on the shore like a horde of locusts. They lingered amongst the opium dens, brothels, and bars that decorated the outskirts of the city.

Malcolm's first act, once they had arrived in Hong Kong, was to bribe the quartermaster to send news back to Jameson & Brixton Company that the ship had never reached port. The first night, while dealing with nausea from land sickness, Malcolm allowed himself to think about his wife. He gave control of the ship to O'Hanlon and walked around the streets of the city. He found an outdoor market and rested for a moment in an empty stall.

Initially, Malcolm found solace in quoting his favorite passages from the bible. The yellowed pages of the book of Job renewed his endurance. Though he tried, he could no longer remember his wife's face or the sound of her voice. He ran from the waters deep into the woods until his lungs burned, and his arms bled from scraping branches. He emerged on the top of a hill and looked back onto the lights of the harbor.

He could no longer conjure his most cherished memory of his wife singing, "A Stor Mo Chroi." Overcome by the tremendous sense of loss, he was beckoned and gave in to the siren's call. Opium soon became his master. He lost touch with reality and was condemned to live in a fog of manufactured pleasure. The smoke entered his lungs, blunted all emotion, and dissolved his memories.

For the second time in his life, fate intervened. Malcolm was dragged from the lightless catacomb amidst his stupor. He was bathed, shaved, and made presentable for Three Finger Tang. He'd been taken aboard a series of interconnected sampans and had been placed before two men. The older one, introduced as Tang, sat cross-legged, and smoked a pipe. The younger one, Tang's son, stood.

"You are an instrument," Tang's son offered. "You need to be played by the right hands, to be effective," he added.

Tang's son was handsome bordering on androgynous. He'd been schooled abroad.

"I'm afraid you've been mistaken," Malcolm said and ran his fingers through his now neatly trimmed beard. He heard the demon's first whisper of withdrawal course through his body, and he shifted around where he sat.

"We'll see," Tang's son said.

Tang's son looked to his father, who'd nodded and extinguished his meerschaum. Tang's son removed something from his pocket and lobbed it over to Malcolm who caught it. Malcolm recoiled at the sight of his wife's locket and sank to the deck. He wailed until Tang's disciples picked him up and brought him onto the shore. For three straight days, Malcolm was consumed by the strain of withdrawal which pushed him to the brink. On the fourth day, after his strength had returned, Malcolm arose in the cold air of the early morning and boarded a vessel to meet with Tang. The man stared out onto the water. Tang finally acknowledged Malcolm's presence, and he held out his hand which contained Malcolm's wife's locket.

"You should not so easily part with such a priceless treasure," Tang said. Momentarily, Malcolm was taken back by Tang's flawless English. Malcolm took the locket and thanked the man. Tang blew smoke from his nose and spat over the side into the water. Malcolm looked down at his white-knuckled fist. He vowed the locket would never leave him again.

"I feel I've no purpose anymore," Malcolm said.

"Then we shall find you some," Tang replied.

THE RAILWAY STRIKE OF 1877, PITTSBURGH, PA

Ridley had set up that morning to extricate Dranoff from his transport to the gallows. Dranoff sported some purple discolorations on his face; Ridley couldn't tell whether he'd gotten that during the melee at the saloon or afterward from the authorities. Ridley had already assembled his weapon by the time Dranoff and his captors had left the jail cell. They all mounted horses, including Dranoff whose hands were tied in front of him.

The aftermath of the war had been a difficult time for both of them, but it had been particularly hard for Dranoff who had drifted from town to town during this reconstruction era and never found solid footing. Eventually, Dranoff had found work as a doorman at a brothel, but it wasn't long before he'd killed a patron and drew the ire of too many connected people. He managed to squeak by for a while until he'd engaged in fisticuffs with the senator's nephew.

Ridley had come to town only a day previously, looking for Dranoff. Had Ridley taken any more time to make up his mind to visit Dranoff, he would have found the man swinging.

The men on the horses began a slow trot just as Ridley

brought the weapon up to his shoulder. Ridley steadied his breathing, took aim, and fired. It took a little under a second for the impact, dead center of the first rider whose head snapped to the side. The man slid from the saddle. The horse, now without a rider, broke into a gallop and was soon gone. The other riders, on horses, drew pistols and slowly looked around.

Ridley reloaded and fired again. This time, he struck the last man in the neck. He must have hit an artery. The man's neck erupted like a geyser. The man stayed in the saddle and flailed around, much to the chagrin of the horse who began to buck until he threw the rider. At this point, it finally dawned on the rest of them they were dealing with a long-range attack from a gifted sharpshooter.

There were two left aside from Dranoff. The remaining men dismounted and decided to return to the safety of the jail. While they were disembarking from their steeds, Dranoff had freed himself from his bonds, dismounted, and retrieved the sidearm from one of the downed men. He shot the two remaining officers in quick succession.

One of the horses galloped away and dragged the body of the man who was still tangled in the saddle. The other horse had fallen with its rider still intact. The man had not been killed by the projectile. Now, as he lay there, the man issued threats of revenge and damnation at Dranoff who slowly walked over and shot the man point-blank.

MALCOLM TRACKED DOWN O'HANLON AND discovered him in bed with four women. All of their limbs were intertwined. O'Hanlon stirred. He was a mighty Grizzly bear coming to life again after a winter of hibernation. His eyes came into focus.

"Christ, I thought you was dead," O'Hanlon said and stretched. The women awoke and quickly fled.

"I was," Malcolm said. "I've got a job for you."

O'Hanlon yawned and grabbed the remnants of whatever foul concoction he'd been drinking the previous evening. He took a healthy pull and sucked the residue from his beard.

"Well," O'Hanlon said.

He cuffed Malcolm on the shoulder and almost knocked him off his feet. Much of their old crew had dispersed long ago. Some had signed on to other expeditions or met their end after indulging in reckless impulses. However, enough of them had remained in Hong Kong, and after allegiances were revived, they commenced to work.

They rechristened their ship as *The Ajax* and subsequently ran and protected goods for Three Finger Tang. At the time, the sea had often teamed with undesirables, so they were busy. The crew met with hostile forces on almost every voyage. Malcolm spared lives when he could and took them when he had to do so. He became adept with a fighting iron and studied the martial arts with Tang's son. He assumed more and more of the local customs until he soon grew into the life, but he had still felt hollow. He focused almost exclusively on his work for Tang and hoped salvation lay somewhere close by.

The majority of their journeys were back and forth to Macau, a Portuguese colony that was a stone's throw away from Hong Kong. Opium was the primary cargo; it made its way from India to Macau and was dispersed throughout Asia for mass consumption. Macau wasn't a dangerous place, but temptation lurked everywhere. It practically breathed down Malcolm's neck. He broke into sweats frequently and was plagued by fever dreams of the past. Though he'd rid himself of his vile habit, he could sometimes feel the smoke in his lungs every time they brought the poppy flowers aboard.

Macau was a frequent destination even when they were not working as the newly built racetrack brought enormous crowds from all over. It was one of O'Hanlon's life's pleasures to play the horses, and soon he spoke about little else. Often, he could be heard lamenting over a sordid affair in which his horse had just failed to win. The Portuguese had dubbed him El Gigante Rojo, and he became a legendary patron of the track. Once, while in a drunken stupor, he was arrested for nearly crippling a jockey who he felt had not tried his hardest to win. Malcolm needed to call in a favor from Tang himself, as well as pay a hefty bribe, to have O'Hanlon released from his cell.

"I guess I owe you again," O'Hanlon had said while he shielded his eyes from the brightness once they got outside of the jail.

"I don't want this to become a habit with you," Malcolm had said.

O'Hanlon was not the sort to readily admit he'd committed an error in judgment, but he nodded in agreement, and for the rest of his sojourns to the track, he kept his transgressions to a minimum. While the crew indulged their vices when they were in Macau, Malcolm would often attend mass instead. The Jesuit priest who oversaw the procession, and conducted the service, was a jolly man given to much laughter. Often Malcolm would linger behind in the emptiness of the cathedral to light a candle in the memory of his wife. One afternoon, as he watched the candle burn, he tried to decipher any symbols in the flame. He felt the Jesuit's presence by him.

"She forgives you, amigo."

Malcolm turned and scrutinized the man before him. The priest had profoundly tanned and creased skin. He displayed a smile, which resonated with pure joy. The Jesuit's vestments overflowed from his gut. However, underneath the jovial manner, Malcolm felt the intensity come off the man in waves, the type reserved for those who'd witnessed pain and death up close.

"Your wife," the Jesuit added.

Malcolm went back to the flame.

"How did you know?"

The man placed his hand on Malcolm's shoulder.

"Unfortunately, I've seen that look on people's faces too many times. Tell me amigo, when was the last time you had confession?"

Malcolm was surprised at himself that he didn't put up a struggle. They stepped into the booth, and the priest drew back the partition and said the words. Once Malcolm began, the memories poured forth as if the dam within him had broken. He uttered long-winded diatribes of deeds and misdeeds which included his misfortune and journey from the cold rains of his homeland in Europe to the never-ending humidity of Asia. The

Jesuit never interrupted. When Malcolm was done, neither of them spoke for a while.

"Walk with me," the Jesuit said, and they both emerged into the sunlight from the cool shadows of the cathedral. Malcolm expected a sermon and braced himself for a fable in which he'd hear about a man who wrestled with similar demons as Malcolm had, only to conquer them with the aid of God.

Instead, the Jesuit led Malcolm along a dirt path away from the city. He paused here and there to comment on the beauty of the land; sometimes, he'd reminisce about his hometown in Portugal, and lament the fact he would probably never see it again.

"Not unlike yourself," the Jesuit intuited about Malcolm's situation.

Before long, they'd gotten to the edge of the water which overlooked a series of small islands that dotted the horizon. The Jesuit motioned for Malcolm to follow, and they negotiated through the dense foliage until they arrived at a dugout that had been hidden among some bushes.

"We must go quickly," the Jesuit began, "If we are to return you to your ship before the morning."

"Where are we going?" Malcolm said.

The Jesuit said nothing, but he had a hardy smile on his face. When they got to the water's edge, Malcolm helped lift the small vessel and deposit it into the water. They didn't have to fight the current, and Malcolm felt at ease being back on the water. Throughout the past few years, he'd grown accustomed to his life as a mariner. The Jesuit proved to be diligent and capable with an oar, and soon they were quickly cutting through the water toward one of the nearby islands. From a distance, Malcolm saw a small collection of poorly constructed bivouacs and shacks near the sand just on the edge of the woods.

Upon the first impressions, the village seemed deserted, a

desolate collection set amidst an untouched landscape. However, though no one was outside, Malcolm sensed people were watching them from the confines of their abodes. He waited for the Jesuit to offer some explanation. When none came, he finally spoke.

"What is this place?" Malcolm said.

The Jesuit turned toward the small village and yelled out something in Cantonese. Though Malcolm didn't understand most of what had been said, he could pick up bits and pieces. Something about not having any fear. A moment went by, and nothing happened. However, Malcolm could smell the sour odor of unwashed bodies and unsanitary conditions. Slowly doors opened, and people assembled. The Jesuit continued to talk to Malcolm while he still waved to the now encroaching masses.

"Some people would call this place Hell, amigo."

THE RAILWAY STRIKE OF 1877, PITTSBURGH, PA

Ridley had already begun to break down his weapon and mount his horse while Dranoff finished with his custodians. Ridley and Dranoff rode away and had been moving ever since. With ongoing labor disputes, they quickly found work.

Ridley ordered another drink. Dranoff began to speak then stopped. His trademark smirk appeared. He took the bayonet from his boot and handed it to Ridley. Ridley accepted the weapon and turned to see who the unfortunate bastard would be who had made the mistake of indulging Dranoff.

The man in question was at the other end of the bar, but it was pretty obvious who it was. The guy was practically boring holes into Dranoff with his staring. The man had a knife scar that went from his upper lip across his cheek, across a discolored eye, and split his eyebrow. The man cracked his knuckles, stood up, and approached. Though it was difficult to be certain, the guy was at least five inches taller and looked to be twenty-five pounds heavier than Dranoff.

"This shouldn't take long," Dranoff said. He was already up and out of his seat.

SOUTH CHINA SEA, 1875,
AFTERMATH OF THE SECOND
OPIUM OR ARROW WAR

THE PEOPLE WERE TENTATIVE IN THEIR APPROACH. Their fear of Malcolm was apparent, and most of them wouldn't stray far from the sanctuary of their hovels.

"How often do you come out here?" Malcolm asked.

"Whenever I can," The Jesuit said.

By now, children had scattered from behind their parents and had run over toward the Jesuit. They had wrapped their arms around his legs, and he dragged them with him further inland.

"Come, we've much to do," the Jesuit said to Malcolm.

Malcolm followed, and he spotted more children. The bravest of them tugged at the Jesuit's pant leg and ran away before he could respond. Malcolm smiled and stayed close, though his instincts were to do otherwise. He drew up to the Jesuit who was speaking with an elder man, probably the leader of this community.

The man's face had been ravaged by leprosy. His body had been deformed to the point where he had to be pushed in a wheelbarrow. The Jesuit knelt and took what was left of the man's hand in his own as if he were greeting a ruling vassal.

While they conversed, the group went back to hanging clothes to dry or preparing food for dinner.

Most of the children had lost interest in their new guests and instead took to playing a game, which seemed to have no rules. Across the way, still partially hidden in the trees, Malcolm glimpsed a figure whose face was covered by a mask.

"Like King Baldwin," the Jesuit said after he had noticed. "The leper king."

Malcolm broke from his trance. He didn't know how long he'd been mesmerized by the figure who seemed to have some supernatural quality. The Jesuit wiped the sweat from his brow with an embroidered handkerchief.

"I have a favor to ask of you," the Jesuit said.

THE RAILWAY STRIKE OF 1877, PITTSBURGH, PA

Laird Shaughnessy had permanent red cheeks and a white beard, not to mention, he was an overweight fellow. He swirled a glass of Cognac and smoked a cigar the circumference of a half dollar. He'd exhale a purple-tinted cloud of smoke along with another deep chortle. Shaughnessy had merged his transportation company with the Pennsylvania Railroad, and he was in town to make sure this potential strike didn't get out of hand. The man next to him, Bill Deckard, had a permanent grimace as if he'd just eaten something which had disagreed with him.

Deckard was also in town on behalf of the board to see the strike didn't go the way of some of the others like West Virginia. If things could be settled peaceably, then so be it. If blood needed to be shed, well, that was why they had hired Ridley and Dranoff.

"Hiram Monroe," Deckard slid a photo across the desk. Both Ridley and Dranoff had been seated in desk chairs and now stood to get a better look.

Monroe was the bespectacled orator from the previous afternoon. According to Shaughnessy, Monroe was a socialist disruptor who was looking to incite a riot. The decision had been reached to remove Monroe from the scene. The police and the various militias had begun to side with the workers, so the National Guard had arrived that morning with the hope to quell the uneasiness.

Monroe had been scheduled to speak at a rally tomorrow.

SOUTH CHINA SEA, 1875,
AFTERMATH OF THE SECOND
OPIUM OR ARROW WAR

GRID HAD BEEN BORN IN THE NEW WORLD TO A Chinese mother and one of her many patrons. She'd been told to terminate the pregnancy, but she had kept it for too long. If they tried anything at this point, she might have been permanently injured, and she was her boss's best earner. So, her son had been born in one of the backrooms.

The boy's leprosy had taken hold of him almost immediately. He found no sanctuary in the brothel, so he was relegated to the streets. He had been beaten frequently and called a living embodiment of sin. Due to his lineage, the words heathen and savage usually followed. Soon, his body bore the scars of their hatred. Being able to remain hidden and silent became his greatest strength, and soon he could move unobserved. It wasn't long before he became a capable thief.

At the age of twelve, on the outskirts of town, he witnessed a raid by an Ohlone war party. They rode without saddles. The tribe released war cries, which frightened the boy and seemed to harmonize with the wails of their victims. The swift annihilation of the same people who'd caused the boy so much pain, and misery, was a revelation to him.

He followed the victors back out into the desert, and that evening slipped past the sentry. He stole some of their weapons. Over the next few years, through the sheer necessity of survival, he spent all of his time developing his skill with a knife and hatchet.

The entirety of his life was fraught with hardship, but occasionally he found hospitality. Sanitariums and hospitals became his refuge. He would walk freely through the hallways, and often he would hear the suffering exhalations of those dying of tuberculosis. The administrators treated him well, but usually, he also sensed their apprehension. Other patients, while delirious, would think him The Grim Reaper, and in his confusion, he chose this as a name for himself after he had misheard it a few times.

Repeated feelings of isolation and stir-craziness would drive him back out into an inhospitable world. His condition worsened as he aged, to the point where looking at his face would cause strangers to have a visceral reaction. Covering his face became an unfortunate necessity.

He lived in the shadows, took what he needed, and continued to evade the authorities. He was caught by The Man of God while trying to steal food. Distrustful of the generosity which followed, Grid had kept his knife handy the entire evening. He sat at the table in The Man of God's home and ate ravenously until he felt pain. The Man of God did not show any fear even though the knife remained visible the whole time.

Afterward, The Man of God provided Grid with new clothes, money, and a bible. Finally, he asked Grid to remove the soiled hood he wore so that he could see Grid's face. Though he was initially apprehensive, Grid did as he was asked.

THE RAILWAY STRIKE OF 1877, PITTSBURGH, PA

It was a windy morning. There wouldn't be a stage or a pulpit, but the workers had laid claim to a street corner where Monroe would give his speech. A group of them had already jury-rigged a platform, so Monroe would be able to be seen from a block away.

Ridley had set up on top of a neighboring roof. He took some preliminary assessments of the wind. It would only be a distance of a few hundred yards, so it wouldn't be that difficult of a shot. Dranoff would be stationed at the front of the building. Ridley would take the shot, leave his weapon, and join Dranoff. They would blend in with the crowd. Odds were, the workers would probably thin out once bullets had been fired. Although, Ridley had learned to be a contrarian. People often acted differently from how he had assumed they would.

Ridley licked his thumb and felt the wind. He removed some lint from his pocket and let it fall. He watched it get caught up in an eddy and settle on the rooftop by his feet. Ridley hefted the weapon and looked through the scope. He listened to Monroe discuss the Hegelian dialectic as it had been interpreted by Karl Marx. Monroe was a gifted speaker, and had Ridley not been on an assignment, he would have gladly stayed and listened to the man continue to rail against the greed of the bourgeoisie.

Recently, Ridley thought of retiring from the life, and again the sentiment hit him.

He could take up with Poppy if she would still want to make a go of it. Ridley hadn't confided his intention to take up with Poppy, but Dranoff probably knew. Dranoff had suspected Ridley's true feelings back then.

Poppy had been a nurse during the war. Word got to Dranoff about Poppy, and her skill with a rifle, so he arranged to have a demonstration. He asked her to participate in a shooting tournament to bolster troop morale. There would be ten entrants altogether including her and Ridley. The contestants began at twenty-five yards away from the targets and moved back by ten yards after each shot. A bullseye was required to remain in the tournament. By seventy-five yards out, it was just Ridley and Poppy. Eventually, they made it to one hundred-fifty yards before the sun had gotten too low, and Dranoff called the match a draw between the two of them due to poor vision conditions.

Ridley had clearly been impressed with Poppy's ability and revealed as much to her. However, he had not pursued the matter further. As Ridley began to dissemble his weapon, Dranoff spoke to him about Achilles and Penthesilea. Penthesilea had been an Amazonian warrior queen who aided Troy during the Trojan war against the Greeks. Achilles had been the greatest Greek warrior. The two met on the battlefield. In one telling of the story, Penthesilea killed Achilles but Zeus, a God, brought Achilles back to life, and Achilles slaughtered Penthesilea.

Regardless, the two combatants had fallen in love with each other during that brief moment, inspired by each other's ability and prowess on the battlefield. The message was cryptic, but Ridley had understood what Dranoff was suggesting. Ridley asked Poppy if he could see her the next day. She said she had to break in a new yearling colt she'd just purchased. If Ridley wanted to join her, he was welcome to do so. Poppy had not been particularly warm or cool to his solicitation, but the following day began a long courtship which involved Ridley spending the next few days visiting and doting on Poppy. Had Ridley not felt an obligation to see his duty with Dranoff through to the end, he would have stayed with her. She had in fact asked him to remain, but she also understood his commitment to the job.

They stayed together that final night and spoke of a future together. Ridley told her he would return as soon as he'd served his term. She told him she would wait. Leaving her that evening had been one of the more difficult experiences he'd faced. During an ensuing battle, Dranoff saved Ridley's life. Ridley, now indebted to Dranoff, wrote a letter to Poppy indicating as much. Again, she told him to follow through with his decision, and she would be waiting for him. Ridley and Dranoff continued to work together, and though they'd never failed to achieve their objective, Ridley still felt indebted.

Now, however, he believed he had settled his account.

The wind picked up and brought Ridley out of his haze. He aimed and squeezed the trigger. Monroe's speech was interrupted by gurgling, and the man clutched at this neck before falling over to the ground. As Ridley headed toward the stairwell, he heard the commotion as the riot started. Ridley didn't hear any accusations clearly, but the workers had assumed the shot had been fired from The National Guard.

"I HAVE CARED FOR HIM SINCE HE WAS YOUNG," THE
Jesuit said. They were all closer to the masked figure now, and
Malcolm tried not to stare openly. The Jesuit continued to say
how he'd previously had a post in America and brought Grid
with him to Macau.

"I'm sorry, but there's no way," Malcolm said.

"I understand I'm asking a lot of you," The Jesuit said.

"No, I don't think you do," Malcolm began. "Can he understand us?" Malcolm gestured toward Grid.

"Yes, but he is unable to speak." The Jesuit suddenly looked
very tired. "He lost his tongue long ago," the Jesuit added.

The Jesuit began coughing and brought his handkerchief to
his mouth. Before Malcolm could put a hand on the Jesuit's
shoulder, Grid's knife blade was already against Malcolm's
throat. The eyes from beneath Grid's mask were unflinching.

Malcolm did not move; however, he looked down as an indi-
cation his attacker do the same. Grid did so, and Malcolm knew
the figure had caught sight of Malcolm's dagger pressed against
Grid's stomach. Grid backed away and put his knife back in its

sheath. He seemed to acknowledge a mutual understanding and allowed Malcolm to administer aid. The three of them returned to the water. Blood still colored the Jesuit's teeth. His jovial nature which had so effortlessly flowed from the man was now gone. It had been replaced by weariness.

"You are both searching for salvation," the Jesuit said. "You will both be able to help each other."

Back at the port, Malcolm watched from afar as the Jesuit bid farewell to his surrogate son. Grid disappeared into the darkness of the alleyway near the church once they had finished with their goodbyes, and Malcolm walked over to the Jesuit.

"How am I going to find him?" Malcolm said.

"He'll always be around. He hides, like the tarantula. The darkness is his domain." Another coughing fit came. When it abated, the Jesuit added,

"Don't worry. He'll find you."

Malcolm shook the Jesuit's hand. He realized he would probably never see the man alive again. Malcolm returned to his ship. Many of the crew voiced their displeasure at Grid's presence.

However, much to Malcolm's surprise, it was O'Hanlon who spoke in Grid's defense and made a declaration that anyone who had a problem with the new arrangement could take it up with O'Hanlon later on the bow of the ship. His proclamation was met with silence. Soon, the matter was forgotten about entirely.

Upon arriving back in Hong Kong, Malcolm had a meeting with Tang. He navigated through the small makeshift island of sampans, but he never shook the feeling that Grid had been lurking nearby, following him. Tang greeted Malcolm with the usual formalities, and when they were seated, he lit his pipe.

"I have good news for you," Tang began. "An incredible bounty." He produced a manifest bearing an insignia Malcolm didn't recognize.

"What's the ship carrying?" Malcolm said.
Tang exhaled and spat over the side.
"Not what. Whom."

THE RAILWAY STRIKE OF 1877, PITTSBURGH, PA

DRANOFF HAD WATCHED THE WORKERS ACROSS THE way finish setting up for the speech. One of them made an introduction for Monroe, gave Monroe's bona fides, and talked about what they hoped to achieve today. Monroe was suddenly standing next to him. The applause lasted a full thirty seconds before Monroe put his hands up and the crowd quieted. The National Guard had taken position across the way. The soldiers had been instructed to stay vigilant, but as long as the workers were only talking, to stand their ground. If it grew violent, the guardsmen were issued orders to retaliate.

Monroe was a blowhard.

Monroe spoke above the heads of most in the crowd, making references to someone named Hegel, Marx, and something about the workers uniting. However, Dranoff got the sense Monroe knew when he needed to pull back a little. At that point, Monroe would refer to The Bible or mention The Pennsylvania Railroad, and the crowd would enthusiastically respond. It didn't matter to Dranoff. Monroe could have his moment in the sun. Soon, Ridley would quiet the man permanently.

Most likely, after Monroe had been silenced, Ridley and Dranoff would move on to the next mission. They hadn't spoken about the longevity of their arrangement, and every so often, Dranoff got the sense Ridley would be fine hanging up his weapon. Maybe Ridley would get that spread of land he'd talked about and settle down with Violet. Dranoff laughed. Dranoff had entertained the idea of hanging it up himself, but it never stuck. He needed to be able to satiate his violent tendencies without fear of reprisal. Perhaps, Dranoff would return to his previous job as a marshall for Judge Isaac Chamberlain.

Chamberlain presided in Alma, Colorado. Recently inducted into statehood in the Union, Chamberlain had been appointed to keep law and order and rarely showed any mercy. While Chamberlain had developed the reputation as a hanging judge, he was happy to let Dranoff be the exterminating angel. As long as justice was served, Chamberlain didn't care who pulled the trigger. Dranoff remembered the last time he wore the badge before Ridley had sought him out.

Dranoff strode into the saloon and had to immediately side-step the melee borne from a poker player accusing another one of cheating. The table had overturned seconds before Dranoff's arrival, but as soon as Dranoff had stepped through the door-way, he was almost knocked over.

At first, two men threw reckless fists at each other while also trying to get a decent hold of the other. Soon, they were joined by other patrons who attempted to break them up. Dranoff continued toward the bar. Along the way, he was propositioned by a woman who had cinched a corset so tight around her midsection Dranoff didn't know how she stayed upright. An off-tune piano spat out a waltz. The man at the keys had had a few drinks already and dissonant notes crept into the song. While it would have derailed most musicians, the piano player soldiered through, creating a new rendition of the song.

Dranoff turned and put his elbows on the bar.

"Hep you?" The bartender said. The man almost had to yell to be heard over the sound of the commotion from both the angry poker players and the piano.

"Rye!" Dranoff said over his shoulder. He turned around as the bartender was pouring his drink. Ridley laid money on the countertop, took the shot, and thanked the man. Dranoff pushed away from the bar and walked toward the corner of the room where Jimmy Floyd and Wayne Dooley had been playing cards with three others. Dooley looked up, saw Dranoff, and went for his Colt Dragoon. Dranoff had a two-gun rig, and at close range, he was equally proficient with both hands. He favored Remington Model '58's, which allowed for the entire cylinder to be removed for a quick, fully loaded replacement.

Before Dooley's weapon could leave its holster, Dranoff had already shot him multiple times. Dooley's chest looked like someone had typed Morse code; he fell out of his chair onto the ground. The piano and fistfight stopped. The thunderclap from the ignited projectiles eventually faded as sound returned.

Floyd began to beg for his life. Ridley held both smoking pistols toward the ceiling, and calmly explained he was serving a writ on behalf of Judge Isaac Chamberlain. Slowly, people returned to their games. Dooley's body continued to bleed out on the saloon floor. Floyd's teeth chattered as he followed Dranoff's instructions to drag Dooley's body outside.

Outside now, Floyd had begun to moan. The fight had been driven from him if it had been there, to begin with. Floyd and Dooley had been wanted for mostly petty crimes. For example, being two-bit players in the recent fence-cutting wars that had sprung up. However, they had robbed a general store that doubled for a post office which made it a federal crime. Therefore, they would stand trial for Judge Chamberlain.

Chamberlain would make a spectacle of pretending to be upset with Dranoff for meting out Dooley's fate. The judge would probably quote Exodus or Deuteronomy, and Dranoff would look solemn as the judge continued his lecture. Of course, it was all for show. Dranoff could serve his writs with full discretion as long as Chamberlain could demonstrate to his voters that he was upholding law and order.

SOUTH CHINA SEA, 1875,
AFTERMATH OF THE SECOND
OPIUM OR ARROW WAR

NO ONE MOVED. EVEN THE MORTALLY WOUNDED seemed to cease their shrieking. The woman motioned for Malcolm to holster his weapon. He did and gave the same instructions to his crew. Such a dark scene had been intruded upon by something so pure. No one in the crew interrupted her. Malcolm ordered Grid and O'Hanlon to see to it survivors were allowed to return to port and anyone who wished to join their crew could.

"I don't like this," O'Hanlon said once he and Malcolm were back in the captain's quarters on *The Ajax*. For her protection, the woman had been taken with them. She currently sat on the floor and stared into space. She had an ethereal quality.

Malcolm strode over to three wooden chests which were partially obscured by his writing-table. He flipped the lid of the first one open and revealed an assortment of coins and precious stones.

"Will this help you sleep better tonight?"

O'Hanlon's eyes widened.

"Forget what I said," he began, "Just for curiosity's sake—"

42

"There are six others when we deliver her to Tang," Malcolm said and gestured to the woman.

O'Hanlon started to laugh. It turned into a deep guttural howl. He exited, and Malcolm closed the lid on the chest. He watched the woman for a moment. Her eyes were closed, and she rocked rhythmically with the swaying of the boat. Malcolm removed his pistol and lay it on the writing desk which had been covered with maps and charts.

He took up his leather-bound ship's log, made some quick notations of the events of the day, careful to note times and details, partially so he would be more accurate in his report to Tang. Above him, he heard O'Hanlon bark orders at the crew and promised them extra servings of grog if they were able to adhere to his timetable. Malcolm stole glances at the woman when he inked his quill. On each occasion, his heart beat a little faster. Malcolm closed the book. She still hadn't moved.

"I wish to thank you," she said in flawless English without opening her eyes. "You have saved me from unbearable solitude."

RAILWAY STRIKE OF 1877, PITTSBURGH, PA

By the time Ridley had made it downstairs to the street, a melee had erupted between the striking workers and The National Guard. Workers armed with rocks threw them at the guardsmen and attempted to wrest the rifles from them.

Though they had a Gatling gun with them, the guardsmen had not employed it. Instead, they had used their bayonets and shot at least twenty in the crowd.

It wouldn't be long before word spread throughout the city and a full-fledged riot ensued. The workers were already at their breaking point. This would send everyone over the edge. Ridley had begun to move when Dranoff grabbed his elbow. Dranoff nodded toward the Gatling gun.

"It's on wheels."

Before Ridley could say he was unarmed, Dranoff had already given Ridley the butt end of one of his Remington '58s.

MALCOLM TWIRLED THE QUILL IN HIS NOW INK-stained fingers. He debated the merits of his situation. He had no idea of Tang's intentions, but that could wait. For now, even keeping the woman on the boat would be an impossibility. She had revealed her name to be Ah Lam, and she had told Malcolm of her situation. She had been part of an arranged marriage. Sadness seemed to weigh her down until it tugged at each fiber of her being. She stared at the floor of the ship, unable to look Malcolm in the eye.

"My intended husband will send his men to the farthest reaches to look for me."

Malcolm waited for her to continue. Tears began to cascade down her cheeks, but she didn't give in to the emotions. Her voice remained steady.

"I am a possession," she added.

Malcolm put down his book and quill and stood up.

"You will be safe here," he said. He walked outside on the deck. The sea air had a corrosive quality to it. He watched his men perform their tasks as the wind whipped through the sails. O'Hanlon was busy giving orders. He pointed with his massive cudgel as he spoke. O'Hanlon spotted Malcolm out of the corner of his eye, and he barked the last command. He sauntered over to join his captain.

"I don't quite know the whole thing," Malcolm said, "but if she's worth half of what I think she is, we're in for more trouble than I can imagine," Malcolm said.

O'Hanlon rubbed at his beard.

"I didn't sign on to be bored," O'Hanlon replied.

He touched Malcolm on the shoulder and went to his post. Malcolm returned to his quarters. Ah Lam had fallen asleep in his desk chair. Malcolm picked her up and moved her to his cot. He continued to write by candlelight. He debated and weighed various outcomes well into the evening. Ultimately, he resigned himself to sleep when it finally came for him. He awoke to her touch. At first, he was disoriented and said his wife's name.

"No," Ah Lam said in response. She placed her hand on his chest.

Neither of them spoke after that. He could not fathom her motives, nor did he care to understand. He held her close to him and was exorcized of his angst. When it was through, they lay together in silence. Malcolm felt his wife's locket around his neck. It was now worn and scratched. He waited for guilt to consume him, but it never came.

"Where is she?" Tang had asked for a second time.

Malcolm kept silent. Then, he finally spoke.

"Safe," Malcolm said.

Tang rattled off a string of profanities.

"You do not think I can find her? You think you can hide her with your red giant and the faceless man? That I will not have you broken and castrated like the beast of burden you are?"

When Malcolm didn't acknowledge Tang's anger, the man took a different approach.

"What do you care what happens to this woman? Her disappearance allows for my business to thrive."

"I've never asked anything of you. I am asking you now," Malcolm said.

"The pawn does not get to give orders to the king," Tang said.

Tang produced his meerschaum and lit the bowl. He flicked the match overboard. The water was so calm, Malcolm thought he'd heard the flame extinguish. Tang yelled something in Cantonese to some of his men stationed on sampans further toward the shore. It was too fast for Malcolm to understand what had been said.

Suddenly, the boat he and Tang was on separated from the island chain. They floated on the open water, but they stayed close to the shoreline. As was customary, Malcolm had surrendered his weapons before boarding.

Now, when some of Tang's men approached him, Malcolm instinctively went for his pistol but clutched at an empty holster. He got in one or two good shots but was subdued. One of Tang's men hit Malcolm in the stomach and knocked the wind out of him. While Malcolm was on his knees, one of them took his wife's locket. They kicked Malcolm in the ribs for good measure. Afterward, they dragged him and deposited him in front of Tang. Up close the old man's face was covered in liver spots. Long, black-and-white hairs dotted his chin. Someone handed the locket to Tang. The old man's bony fingers wrapped around the silver casing. Long and yellowed nails enveloped it until it disappeared. Tang blew smoke out through his nose.

"You may think you have control of your life," Tang began.

He stretched out further until he was almost supine. He flung the locket over his shoulder into the water; Malcolm heard an audible plop as the jewelry sank.

"More importantly, you no longer have value," Tang said

Tang's men surrounded Malcolm. They had their weapons drawn. Malcolm, still on his knees, raised his hand in the air to give a signal. Immediately, he slunk down and covered himself. The incoming arrows hit all four of Tang's men in the sternum and back. The wind picked up, and Malcolm stood.

"My friends are pretty adept with a bow," Malcolm began, "even from this distance."

He took the knife from the hand of one of Tang's dead subordinates and waved toward the shore to let Grid and O'Hanlon know he was safe. Tang grew rigid in his posture; his face betrayed nothing.

"Put out your left hand," Malcolm ordered. Malcolm knelt, so he squatted in front of the old man. Tang lay his hand out on the deck. The three stumps on his hand had calloused over and ended in a latticework of scars.

"Most importantly," Malcolm said, as he brought the knife down,

"You're going to have to change your name."

DEFENSE OF THE GARRISON, 1878

P OPPY THREW HER APPLE CORE AND WATCHED A POLLO, her Halls Heeler, scamper after it. Apollo had been sired from Colossus, an Australian Cattle Dog, basically, a cross between a border collie and a dingo. Poppy's father Ignatius had been a prominent cattleman and had heard about the effectiveness of the Halls Heeler. Initially, Halls himself had only bred the dogs for his family. When Halls passed away, and his dog's litters were made public, Ignatius was eager to get a few.

Colossus used to keep the cattle in line by nipping at their heels. It was how his breed had gotten its name. When Ignatius passed, and Poppy inherited the herd, she sold the cattle since she did not want to administer his estate. She subsequently took the money and bought the apple orchard. She had a knack for gardening and horticulture and knew it would be a great enterprise. She bought a few acres in Colorado and occupied a ranch that had been used to house soldiers during Westward expansion. Of course, Apollo came with her. While there weren't cattle for him to herd, he kept the coyotes at bay. Poppy could hold her own with the Winchester repeating rifle, but Apollo had been a natural deterrent.

She watched Apollo take the apple core and return it dutifully at her feet. She picked it up, threw it, and watched him race after it.

"Violet."

Ridley stood twenty feet away. Violet had been a nickname Poppy had earned during her youth from her favorite type of flowers. Ridley was the only person who still called her that. She picked an apple from the tree closest to her and threw it at him. He had not been prepared, and it hit him in the chest.

"Still deadly," he said and massaged his sternum.

She laughed. Apollo dropped the apple and jogged over to Ridley who bent down and scratched Apollo's back.

Ridley and Dranoff had shown up at the ranch the day before. Poppy had told them they were more than welcome to stay for a few days. Dranoff said he was going to continue to Alma. He had sent a telegram to a Judge Chamberlain to see if he could be employed as a marshall. The judge had enthusiastically welcomed Dranoff back into the fold. Ridley had hinted he would love to take Poppy up on her offer to stay.

Poppy gathered up her hair, red, the color of cinnamon, and put it in a bun on her head which she held in place with an ornate butterfly pendant. She gave a quick whistle, and Apollo darted from underneath Ridley.

"Let's go," she said to Ridley and started walking back to the house. "I received word my brother will be here tomorrow," she added.

SAN FRANCISCO, 1878

"TWIN SISTER?" MALCOLM SAID.

Malcolm, O'Hanlon, Grid, and Ah Lam had been in San Francisco for a few weeks. There was a vibrant Chinese community, so it would be easier for Ah Lam to acclimate. In fact, Ah Lam had settled in well and found work at a theater. She was content to stay in San Francisco. She had assumed a new identity and was looking forward to a bright future. However, O'Hanlon, Grid, and Malcolm were already tiring of city life. Not to mention, it would only be a matter of time before word got back to Tang about their current location. They were too distinct looking of a group to be able to disguise themselves.

While Malcolm certainly had had the opportunity to kill Tang, the man was still a venerated leader who ran the ports. Had Malcolm rid the world of Tang, it would have been akin to signing his own death warrant. As it was, Malcolm took the rest of the fingers from Tang's hand.

Malcolm took a sip of his tea.

O'Hanlon had mentioned he'd had a twin sister who lived in Colorado and would be able to offer them hospitality.

"What's her name?" Malcolm asked.

"Poppy," O'Hanlon began. O'Hanlon and his sister had grown up in an affluent family. His father Ignatius had built an empire as a cattle baron. However, while Poppy had taken to life on the ranch, becoming proficient at riding and shooting, O'Hanlon had been more interested in the water.

"Probably because I grew up away from the ocean," O'Hanlon said.

O'Hanlon had had thoughts on joining the Navy but ended up joining a whaling ship and becoming a sailor. He ambled around from crew to crew until he ended up on *The Emerald*.

"What about The Merchant Marines or Jem Mace?" Malcolm asked.

"Don't believe everything you hear," O'Hanlon said and grinned.

DEFENDING THE GARRISON, ALAMOSA, COLORADO, 1878

IT TOOK THEM TWO DAYS TO GET TO ALAMOSA. ALONG the way, Malcolm decided he would head south through Texas to Mexico after they left Poppy's ranch. Grid would accompany him, but O'Hanlon said he might head back to California and see if he could become part of a ship's crew again.

At some point, O'Hanlon would be the captain of a vessel. Being tied to the land wasn't for him. They happened upon Poppy's orchard early in the afternoon. Poppy had been outside with her dog and an affable-looking fellow. The horses stopped. Poppy recognized her brother.

"Phineas!" she said and broke off in a run. The dog, not certain how to act with the strangers, but realizing his owner was happy, also took off in a run.

"Phineas?" Malcolm said quietly.

O'Hanlon shot Malcolm a glance. Malcolm put both his hands in the air as if to suggest he wasn't going to make a big deal about it. Poppy embraced her brother. Grid had already dismounted and was tending to his horse's hoof. The dog was enthralled with Grid and slowly approached him.

Poppy stopped her hug and stared at the masked man and Apollo. The dog was on his back while the man rubbed Apollo's stomach. Apollo was certainly friendly, but she had never seen him immediately give up his belly like that to a stranger. Poppy tried to say as much, but instead, her mouth opened and closed without emitting a sound. She took a step back.

"Grid has a way with animals," Phineas's other friend said and walked closer.

"I'm Malcolm by the way," he added.

"Poppy. Nice to meet you."

"Likewise," Malcolm said.

The man named Grid stood and walked over to the group. Apollo followed at Grid's heels and surveyed the other new strangers. Satisfied no one posed a threat, Apollo disappeared further into the orchard. Ridley joined the group too. Everyone was introduced to each other. Poppy suggested they all return to the house to get better acquainted, and they could have something to eat.

Up close, Ridley could see the resemblance between the siblings. Some of the indications were obvious: hair color, and certain word pronunciations. However, some were more subtle like the way the light refracted from their noses.

Poppy told everyone to take a spot in the parlor while she made preparations for lunch. Ridley reminded her to set a place for Dranoff who would be by to retrieve the Gatling gun. Poppy said she would. Poppy employed a staff of caretakers who would work the orchard field and maintain the estate. They would take care of preparing everything. She excused herself, returned a few minutes later, and took a spot next to Ridley on a couch.

The masked man who didn't speak stood in the corner. He was alert and his eyes remained focused even when the conversation drifted. Poppy's brother, Phineas, took a seat opposite her and Ridley. He seemed eager to catch up about Poppy's life over the last few years. Ridley got the sense Phineas was a bombastic fellow with whom Ridley would get along. Still, Ridley didn't know how Phineas would react to the idea Ridley had planned on proposing marriage to Poppy.

Malcolm was a little more difficult to read. Malcolm was seated in a chair next to Phineas, with his back to a wall, and Ridley noticed every so often Malcolm's right hand would hover over the handle of his revolver as if he was calmed by its presence.

***

Malcolm saw a side of O'Hanlon he'd never seen before, and it intrigued him. The man seemed more vulnerable in front of his family. Still, something was disconcerting which Malcolm couldn't quite put his finger on, and he remained uneasy. Malcolm got the sense Ridley was more interested in impressing O'Hanlon. The siblings continued to catch up when the conversation was interrupted by the whinnying of horses and the dog barking outside.

"Must be Dranoff," Ridley said and excused himself. He returned a moment later with a new guest.

Dranoff wore a long duster and a Stetson; Malcolm had never met a marshall before, but he imagined Dranoff was the prototype. Dranoff carried with him a levered rifle and wore a walrus-style mustache. Dranoff gladly shook hands with everyone, including Grid, and quickly made himself at home on an ottoman near the couch. He'd only been sitting for less than a minute when the conversation was again interrupted by the dog's non-stop barking.

"Expecting anyone else?" Malcolm said.

"No," Poppy replied. She stood and went to the window.

Poppy had been relieved the two groups of friends were getting along as well as they were. She hadn't asked Phin how long he and his friends would be staying, but it would be nice to have them around.

Looking out the window, she saw a group of people slowly approaching the house: members of The Order of the Unfinished Soul. They were a Pentecostal church who lived an isolated existence on a commune a mile away. Each wore garments with symbols depicting their religious order. Most people in the town had labeled them a cult. The members never left the sanctuary of their commune which allowed for gossip to spread easily about their activities. Some townsfolk had proffered the cult performed animal sacrifices, worshipped pagan gods, or were cannibals. Many of the rumors were in direct conflict with others.

Poppy didn't care one way or the other. The members kept to themselves. She never heard or saw any of them except if she rode by their commune. Now, they looked dazed or drunk. A few of them were disheveled and appeared to have been wounded. She saw Alfonse, one of her caretakers, come around from the side of the house and address the group. Poppy couldn't hear what he had said, but all the members turned their head in unison when he got their attention.

A woman with a torn dress, who was leading the group, put her hands up. When she got about ten feet away from him, Alphonse turned to run. He moved toward the house but tripped on a tree root. Alphonse rolled onto his back just as she fell on top of him.

Poppy watched Alphonse violently shake as the woman

smothered him. Her head bobbed a few times, then the woman looked up and her face was covered in blood. She had bitten Alphonse in the neck.

"Ray?" Poppy said. Immediately, the fellow Ridley, who'd been sitting next to her was up and beside her at the window. Her voice had broken.

"It's alright, Violet," Ridley said.

"Violet?" Phineas said. He wrinkled his brow.

"Let me get the Winchester," Ridley said to Dranoff, who tossed the weapon without saying anything. Dranoff was up and made his way over to the window which prompted the rest of them to gather. The window looked out on the vast expanse of the front of the estate. The orchard was in the distance. Walking toward the house, at a slow pace, were about twenty people in various states of undress. Some had wounds to their body that should have killed them outright. One person had a hatchet buried in his chest. One of them looked like a ravenous animal feeding on a corpse. The dog continued to bark, but it maintained a healthy distance between itself and the oncoming group.

Poppy walked to the front door, opened it, and called for Apollo, who dutifully turned and ran to her. Once he was inside, she shut the door and returned to the group. Again, Apollo found Grid and offered his belly. Grid happily obliged the animal. Ridley had opened the window and aimed. Ridley fired a shot that hit one of them in the chest. It made a hole but did little else to slow or stop the person. The other members outside had continued to move closer to the body on the ground. They all knelt and began to feed.

"Jesus," Ridley said.

Malcolm's mind swam a mile a minute trying to process what he was seeing outside.

"Is anyone else here?" Malcolm said to Poppy.

"Esmerelda and Dante, but they're both in the orchard." She looked out the window and shuddered.

"We should get her out of here," Malcolm said to O'Hanlon.

"I'm not going anywhere," Poppy said, walking over to the gun rack on the wall, and selecting a Spencer rifle.

"Alright. What do you suggest?" Malcolm said. It could have sounded sarcastic, but his tone was sincere.

"We should take cover in the barn. Fewer doors and windows," Poppy said.

"Then what?" Malcolm asked.

"Then we send them to Hell," Poppy said.

The barn was out back. While there was a clear path between the house and the barn, they would need to move quickly. Legions of the undead were approaching, and though they moved slowly, soon it would be too late.

Ridley and Poppy went out the door first and lay down suppressive fire. The others ran for the barn with Apollo in the lead. Once they had cleared the barn's threshold, both Ridley and Poppy joined them. Both fired a handful of times, and each shot hit the target.

Once inside, Ridley and Dranoff went directly to the Gatling gun, began loading ammunition, and angled it, so it was facing the door.

"What in God's name is happening?" Ridley said and stopped what he had been doing.

Everyone paused as if they just realized they had forgotten to contemplate that question.

"After this is over," Poppy said, suggesting they prioritize their survival first. Then they could discuss what was transpiring.

"Someone slide the door open when we're ready?" Dranoff said.

"I'll do it," Malcolm offered.

"You know," O'Hanlon said to Malcolm, "I never got my rematch."

Poppy climbed to the hayloft. Apollo scampered into a bucket attached to a pully, and she hoisted him up. Collectively, they could all hear the horses whinny from the neighboring stalls. Malcolm and Grid produced their assorted weapons, and O'Hanlon took a scythe from among the equipment leaning against the far wall. When he had finished priming the weapon with Dranoff, Ridley joined Poppy in the loft. Both of them aimed with their rifles.

Malcolm calmed his breathing, readied his firearm, and recalled a discussion he'd had long ago with Tretiak while they had been incarcerated. Malcolm had originally been placed in The Hardtack Side of the prison where thousands of inmates were crammed into a small area along with cadavers and human excrement. For any infraction at all, an inmate might be whipped, tortured with thumbscrews, or made to wear a skullcap vice. Life expectancy on The Side was short. Later, during an audit of prison records, it had been discovered over ten inmates died a day on average.

Thankfully, due to Tretiak's conniving, Malcolm had been housed in a separate section, The Oaken Side. Each inmate had their own room along with other benefits. There was even a barber, a shop, and bar. Now, Malcolm and Tretiak sat at a table in a room which had been converted into a library.

"The Golden Mean," Tretiak had begun. Tretiak's voice had been hoarse. His words were rough due to his accent.

"If you were to think of two extremes," Tretiak had said and drew an imaginary line on the table with his finger.

"At one end you've got cowardice. What's on the other end?" He asked.

Malcolm had licked his lips before he answered.

"Courage?" Malcolm had said.

"No," Tretiak replied.

Malcolm sighed.

"Recklessness," Tretiak said. He traced his finger a few inches back toward the middle of the imaginary line.

"Courage is what we should strive to achieve, but always we are battling between recklessness and cowardice," Tretiak added. Tretiak sat back and sculpted his beard into a point with his thumb and forefinger.

"Someday, you will understand," Tretiak said.

As Malcolm readied himself for battle with the undead, he understood. Malcolm remembered his wife singing, and suddenly he wasn't fearful. He was at peace.

Since it was still afternoon, sunlight streamed in through the cracks in the barn. Crickets had begun to chirp which became a constant sound interspersed with the moaning and movement of the undead.

Grid had once heard a prophecy this day would come. The Man of God had told Grid about how the dead would one day return to the land of the living.

"Everyone ready?" Dranoff asked.

All confirmed they were. Malcolm slid open the barn door.

The mass of the undead had congregated outside and was almost to the entrance.

Dranoff began to crank the handle of the weapon. The Gatling gun roared and mowed down the first few rows of the undead. The weapon was incredible. The rest of them watched in awe as Dranoff finished another revolution. The barrels all smoked and slowly the quiet seeped back into the barn. Dranoff reloaded before the next wave could approach.

"How about we get married if we make it out of this?" Ridley said to Poppy

CAPTAIN'S LOG, THE TIAMAT,
1880

to a combination of not wanting to forget anything he'd been told, and an eagerness to get it all down. He'd received information from another ship that had just returned from the South China Seas.

There was still no explanation as to the re-animation of the dead. Like those who had disappeared from the Roanoke Colony a few hundred years previously, without a trace, there would probably never be an answer.

There have been very few records about The Order of the Unfinished Soul to comb through. They didn't have any religious texts, like a bible, so most of the information about them has been conjecture. However, I will pursue the matter until I meet my end.

As for other news, Ah Lam opened and continues to operate a theater in San Francisco. Three Finger Tang succumbed to an illness. One of his children currently ran the Hong Kong ports, and word was Grid had returned to Macau to become the protectorate of a leper colony. Neither Dranoff nor Malcolm had made it from the barn that day.

The captain stopped writing.

Malcolm had sacrificed himself. The Gatling gun had done its job, but the undead continued to appear. While they discovered shooting them in the head would bring them down, there had been too many. If they stayed and continued to engage, they would have been overwhelmed.

Malcolm suggested the group make a run for it, and he offered to operate the Gatling gun. The group had managed to shut the door. Now, they slid it open, and Malcolm opened fire. Another handful of the undead dropped, and the group of living ran from the barn. Malcolm stopped firing and began singing ""A Stor Mo Chroi." Malcolm walked toward the undead who swarmed him. In doing, he so gave the group enough time to escape. It had been a long time, but the captain broke down crying at the memory. The captain wiped his eyes and picked up a letter that had arrived earlier in the day. He reread it, smiled, and continued to write.

I have not given up hope to discover the cause of what all of us suffered from that day, nor will I ever stop mourning. However, The Tiamat will plot a course to return to the United States post haste for my sister's wedding.

- Captain Phineas O'Hanlon

ACKNOWLEDGMENTS

Thank you, Heather, for reading an earlier draft and providing feedback, Gabi for copyedits, and "Aunt" Carole for too many things to name.

ABOUT THE AUTHOR

Andrew Davie has worked in theater, finance, and education. He taught English in Macau on a Fulbright Grant, at the university level in New York and Hong Kong, and at the middle/high school level in Virginia. Currently, he's pursuing his Clinical Mental Health Counseling Degree, and has survived a ruptured brain aneurysm and subarachnoid hemorrhage.

He has published short stories in various places, a memoir and addendum, and crime fiction books with All Due Respect, Close to the Bone, Alien Buddha Press, and Next Chapter. He also co-hosts a music review show called Happy Hour with Heather and Guest.

To learn more about Andrew Davie and discover more Next Chapter authors, visit our website at www.nextchapter.pub.

From Beyond
ISBN: 978-4-82414-384-6

Published by
Next Chapter
2-5-6 SANNO
SANNO BRIDGE
143-0023 Ota-Ku, Tokyo
+818035793528

17th May 2022

9 784824 143846